This book belongs to

_____

Walt Disney's

Bambi

A Read-Aloud Storybook

Adapted by Liza Baker

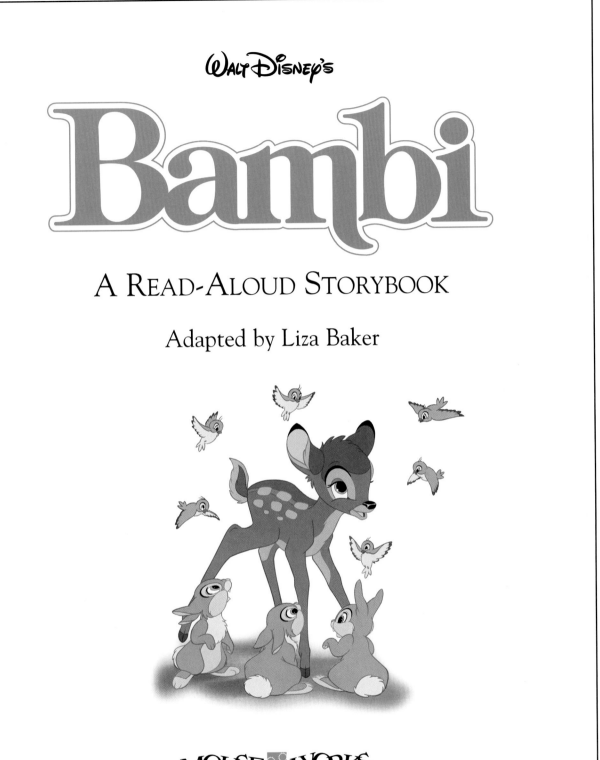

MOUSE WORKS

Find us at www.DisneyBooks.com for more Mouse Works fun!

© 1999 Disney Enterprises, Inc.
The edition containing the full text of *Bambi, A Life in the Woods*
by Felix Salten is published by Simon & Schuster.
Printed in the United States of America.
ISBN: 0-7364-0121-0

Springtime in the Forest

Deep in the forest, Thumper the bunny was spreading exciting news. "A new prince is born!" he shouted.

In a nearby clearing, a mama deer lay with her newborn son.

"This is quite an occasion," said Friend Owl. "It isn't every day a prince is born."

The mama deer named her son Bambi.

Days passed and Bambi began to explore his world. There was so much to see!

"Good morning," called some possums. Bambi turned his head upside down to greet them!

Then a furry creature popped out of the ground. "Good morning!" said the mole. Startled, Bambi tumbled to the ground.

Thumper called out, "Get up! Try again!" Bambi struggled to his feet. He didn't want to miss any of the fun!

9

Every day Bambi's friends showed him new things. "Those are birds," they explained.

"Burr!" repeated Bambi.

"It's burr-duh," corrected Thumper.

"Bird!" said Bambi loudly. The bunnies cheered.

"Bird!" said Bambi again when a butterfly landed on his tail.

Thumper laughed. "No, that's a butterfly!"

Then Thumper introduced his friend to flowers. But as Bambi bent toward them he found himself nose-to-nose with a skunk! "Flower," said Bambi proudly. Thumper giggled but "Flower" was that little skunk's name from then on.

When thunder rumbled, Bambi hurried to his cozy thicket. As he nestled close to his mother, the pitter-patter of rain lulled him to sleep.

Later sunshine filled the sky again and Bambi's mother decided it was time to show him the meadow.

The meadow was so open and green that Bambi
darted forward. But his mother leaped in front of him.
"There may be danger!" she scolded.

Once Bambi's mother was sure it was safe, Bambi
bounded into the field. Suddenly, he heard a "Rrribit!"

Bambi followed the frog until it splashed into a nearby pond. Then Bambi noticed his own reflection and that of a smiling girl fawn.

"That's little Faline," Bambi's mother told him. "Go on. Say hello."

"Hello," he said shyly. Faline giggled and began to chase him. Bambi joined in the game and they played happily in the field. Bambi had found a new friend.

The Great Prince

A thundering herd of stags galloped onto the meadow. The biggest stag stopped and looked at Bambi.

Bambi asked his mother who the stag was. She answered, "He is very brave and wise. He is the Great Prince of the Forest." He was also Bambi's father.

23

Suddenly a gunshot sounded! As the animals scattered, Bambi lost his mother. Instantly, the Great Prince was at Bambi's side. He reunited Bambi with his mother and led them home safely.

Time passed quickly in the forest, and Bambi woke one morning to find the world covered in a soft white blanket. It was his first winter!

Bambi found Thumper skating on the frozen pond. "Come on, Bambi!" Thumper called.

Bambi ran toward the ice. With a sudden *splat*, Bambi slipped onto his belly. And when Thumper tried to teach him how to balance on the ice, Bambi slid them both into a snowbank!

They landed by a small den where Flower lay sleeping. Flower explained that skunks sleep through the winter. "Good night," he murmured.

The snowy days seemed endless, and food grew scarce. "I'm hungry, Mother," said Bambi.

"Winter won't last forever," she assured him.

30

Finally, Bambi saw the first sign of spring—a small patch of grass. Bambi was nibbling at it when a gunshot rang out!

"Run for the thicket!" cried his mother.

Bambi ran as fast as he could. When he reached the thicket he said, "We made it, Mother!" But she wasn't there. Then Bambi heard a second gunshot.

As Bambi cried, the Great Prince appeared before him. "Your mother can't be with you anymore," he said gently. "Come with me, my son." Together, Bambi and his father walked deeper into the forest.

Before long, flowers began to bloom and birds'
songs filled the air. Even Flower awakened from his
long winter's sleep. Spring had arrived!

34

During the winter, Bambi had grown into a handsome buck. And Thumper and Flower had both grown to their full sizes.

When the owl saw them, he said, "It won't be long before you're twitterpated. Nearly everyone falls in love in the springtime." The three friends declared that it would not happen to them!

But when Flower saw a pretty skunk, he happily walked off with her. Then Thumper came across a lovely bunny. When she petted his ears, Thumper's foot went *thump*, *thump*, *thump*.

Lonely, Bambi stopped to drink from a pond. A familiar face looked back at him in the reflection.

"Don't you remember me?" asked a sweet voice. "I'm Faline." Faline the fawn had grown into a beautiful doe!

Together, Bambi and Faline played in the meadow just as they had done the summer before.

Now Bambi understood what Friend Owl meant. He had never felt so happy.

Suddenly an angry stag appeared. "Help!" cried Faline as the stag tried to force her to come with him. Bambi butted the stag with all his strength.

The defeated stag limped away, and from that day on Bambi and Faline were inseparable.

Man Comes to the Forest

Bambi awoke one morning sensing danger. Smoke was in the air and he could see a fire burning.

The Great Prince told him, "It is Man. We must go deep into the forest. Hurry!"

News of the danger quickly spread. Frightened
animals scurried underground or raced deeper
into the forest.

As Faline searched for Bambi, hunting dogs jumped at her from the bushes. "Bambi!" she cried, scrambling to the top of a steep cliff.

The hounds snapped at her heels, barking ferociously. Faline was trapped!

Just then, Bambi sprang out of the woods and charged the dogs with his sharp antlers.

He attacked one dog after another until Faline bounded to safety.

Bambi escaped the dogs but as he leaped after Faline, a gunshot sounded. Wounded, Bambi tumbled to the ground. Fire raged toward him but he couldn't get up. Then he heard the voice of the Great Prince.

"You must get up, Bambi," said the Great Prince. Bambi staggered to his feet. "Follow me," his father said. "We'll be safe in the river."

Soon they came to a waterfall. With nowhere else to turn, they leaped toward the rapids below.

Bambi and the Great Prince finally reached the island where Faline stood waiting. Even as they watched the beautiful forest burn, they all knew that when Man was gone, the animals would bravely rebuild their homes.

Autumn turned to cold white winter and then to spring. "Wake up, Friend Owl!" said Thumper and his four thumping baby bunnies.

"It's happened!" called Flower to the baby skunk scurrying behind him.

The animals circled around the thicket where Faline and her two fawns lay.

"Prince Bambi ought to be mighty proud," said the owl as the fawns opened their big eyes to greet their friendly visitors.

Bambi was now the Prince of the Forest. And as he and his family began their lives together, Bambi thought of the lessons he hoped to teach his children — lessons he had learned from his mother and father long ago.